VICTOR & HUGO
BUNGLERS IN CRIME
THE GREAT TRAIN ROBBERY

written by Jimmy Hibbert
illustrated by Primary Design

Carnival
An Imprint of HarperCollinsPublishers

Hugo drove through yet another red light.
A delivery van carrying a load of *Yumm-me-chunx* dog food swerved to avoid hitting the
mobile headquarters of 'Naughtiness
International', and its rear doors swung
open. Tins of *Yumm-me-Chunx* rolled down
the road.

"Ooh look, Rover," said an old lady to her
dog. "Din-dins!"

"Woof!" barked Rover and, dragging his
owner behind him at the end of his lead, he
set off in hot pursuit of his favourite food.

"But Victor!" Hugo complained, quite
unaware of the chaos he was causing. "It
was not my fault!"

"Oh no?" replied his brother, angrily. "So
who was it who tried to hold up the bank
with a jam doughnut?"

"Well..."

"I said a *gun*, not a bun, you brain of a
biscuit!" raged Victor. "Turn right here."

"Right away, my Victor," said Hugo and
turned the van sharply. To the left.
Straight into a rubbish tip. The van
ploughed through the dump, scattering
empty tin cans, milk cartons, old toothpaste
tubes, potato peelings, cauliflower stalks
and all sorts of other nasty stuff in its wake.

It came to rest in the middle of a sea of evil-smelling rubbish, quite a lot of which had found its way into the van.

"Gordon Bennett!" squawked Interpoll. "What a pong!"

Victor sighed a deep sigh and removed a rather smelly old sock from his face.

"What is the point!" he said quietly to himself.

"The point?" chirped Hugo. "It is a sort of sharp bit at the end of something and if someone sticks it in you, you go ouch!"

4

Luckily for Hugo, at that moment Interpoll rang. (Had he not, Victor was on the point of finding a sharp bit of something to make Hugo go "ouch!") Instead, Victor took Interpoll off his perch and spoke.

"Hello? Victor and Hugo of Naughtiness International, no crime too big, no crime too small, how may I help you?" he enquired in his oiliest tones.

Hugo tugged at Victor's tie. "Who is it, Victor? Who is it?" he asked eagerly.

"Take your hands off my tie!" hissed Victor. "No, no, no, Monsieur, not you. My brother, he is pulling my tie." Victor put out a hand and pulled on Hugo's beret. The beret flumped down over Hugo's face.

"Ooh! It have gone all dark!" Hugo said with great surprise.

"Yes. Now shut up!... No, no, no Monsieur! Not you."

Victor listened intently as the caller told him just what he wanted.

When Victor finally hung up, he turned to his brother and said, "Well, Hugo, my little cabbage. We are going to steal a train."

"A train?" asked Hugo in great excitement. "A big train that goes chuff chuff chuff woo woo choo choo choo?" And he did a fair imitation of a steam train travelling at high speed.

"Yes," said Victor. "A train. Mr X is a railway enthusiast and he wants us to steal a certain train for him. We are to go to Crumbridge in Bassetshire where there is the Tinkerbell Line terminus and there we are to find the steam engine and take it to Mr X who will pay us the large amount of money and we will be rich!"

"Rich!" enthused Hugo.

"Yes. Rich. I will be tall, handsome and rich, and you will be little, stupid and rich."

"Goody! Goody goody gumdrops! Goody gumdrops with big pink bows on! Goody... Just a minute!" Hugo paused.

"Well? What is it?" asked Victor.

"The steam train is very big, yes?" Hugo mused.

"Yes."

"So how do we get it in the van?"

"You fool! You foolish, foolish fool! We drive it!" said Victor.

"We drive the train into the van?" Hugo was puzzled.

"No, no, no, no, no! We drive the train to Mr X."

"Ah! I see! Hee hee!" Hugo became enthusiastic again. "Yippee! I have always wanted to be a train driver!" and resuming his train impressions, he put the van into reverse and backed out of the rubbish dump at high speed.

Crumbridge is a quiet little town nestling at the foot of the Peasmold hills in Bassetshire. It is known to railway buffs as the home of the Tinkerbell Line, one of only three working railway lines served by steam engines in the country.

In Crumbridge station, George Sparkes, the train driver, was shunting the Tinkerbell Belle into a large shed prior to going home for his lunch. The Tinkerbell Belle was a big, shiny, red steam engine; it was, in fact, the very steam engine that Victor and Hugo were intending to steal.

9

As Mr Sparkes put the brakes on to stop
the train, he didn't notice two furtive figures
lurking in the shadows, and as he stepped
down from the footplate, he didn't hear one
of the figures whisper to the other: "Take
your hands off my tie, you brain of a
beetroot!" Nor did he hear, as he closed the
shed doors, the reply: "But Victor! Look! It
is the train!"

"Yes," said Victor, for of course the
figures were none other than Victor and
Hugo. "Yes! I can see that it is the train!
Now, come along!"

10

Victor and Hugo crept stealthily towards the red engine. As they drew closer they realised that the steam engine was a lot bigger than they had bargained for. Still, a job was a job and so they climbed up on to the footplate and into the cab.

"So! Now all we have to do is to drive the train to Mr X!" said Victor, sounding more sure of himself than he actually felt.

"Yes!" agreed Hugo. Then he began to think, which was never an easy thing for him.

After a pause he asked: "How?"

"How?" snorted Victor. "How? Ha! It is simple!"

"Oh. Oh good. So what do we do?"

"Erm... well... we... we... erm..." Victor was stumped for an answer. He peered at the dials and levers and meters and valves in front of him. They didn't seem to offer any clue as to how to start the engine.

"You don't know, do you," said Hugo.

"Of course I know!" lied Victor. "I am just checking the... the controls." He leant over to get a closer look and put his hand on the fire door. The fire door was still very hot as the engine had only recently been driven. Victor leaped into the air.

"Owoooch!" he yelled, and "Aaaarghhh" as he banged his head on the roof of the cab.

"Hmmmn," mused Hugo. "If that is how you drive the train, I do not think I am going to like it."

Victor blew on his burned hand and rubbed his sore head, but his little accident had reminded him how a steam train runs.

"First of all," he said, "we must make the fire."

"Hee hee hee!" giggled Hugo. "Now you are making the joke! Hee hee hee!"

"No, I..."

"Hee hee hee! A fire! We will burn the train!"

"No, we… "

"Hee hee hee!" Hugo fell about the cab, clutching his sides which ached from laughing. Victor, seeing that he would get no sense out of his brother for a minute or two, opened the fire door.

"See?" he said, as the glow of hot embers lit up the dark cab.

"Ooh yes!" Hugo stopped giggling at once. "It is a fire."

"Yes. And we must build it up and make it very hot." said Victor. He found a shovel on the coal tender behind the engine and passed it to Hugo.

"Shovel!" he ordered.

"Yes," agreed Hugo. "That is a shovel."

"No, no, no, no, no!"

"It is not a shovel?" Hugo eyed Victor with suspicion. "It looks like a shovel to me."

"I meant shovel as in 'shovel some coal on to the fire'," Victor said, passing it to Hugo. Hugo took it dutifully and began shovelling coal into the fire box.

Soon the fire was burning hot and bright.

"There!" said Victor. "Now we are ready."

"Good. So what do we do now?" asked Hugo.

"We... erm... ahem," Victor stared at the controls. He had no idea what to do next but he wasn't going to show Hugo that. "We pull this lever," said Victor, as if he'd been driving trains all his life.

"Me! Me!" Hugo jumped up and down with excitement. "I want to pull the lever! Please, Victor? Please can I pull the lever?"

"Oh, very well," Victor agreed, grudgingly. Hugo pulled the lever hard. The train's whistle shrieked and the two brothers almost jumped out of their skins.

"Ssshhh! Be quiet! You will ruin everything!" hissed Victor.

"But Victor, you said that..."

14

"Yes, yes, yes. I know what I said. I made a deliberate mistake. Just to catch you out," Victor lied.

"Ooh! You rotter!"

"Yes. So now we will pull… erm… *this* lever," said Victor.

"Well, this time you can pull it yourself," grumbled Hugo. "I do not want to get the blame when it goes wrong." But to their surprise and relief a loud chuffing and puffing came from the engine and, slowly but surely, the train moved forward.

Outside the shed, George Sparkes was about to cycle home for his lunch. He unlocked his bicycle and put on his cycle clips and…

"What's that?" he muttered, as a faint but familiar noise came to his ears. "Sounds like the whistle!" He shook his head and told himself that he must be imagining things.

"The missus keeps saying as how I should take a holiday," he chuckled. "Perhaps she's..." He stopped to listen again.

No. It couldn't be. It sounded like... it was! With a splintering of timbers, the Tinkerbelle Belle came crashing through the shed doors and roared off down the track, belching steam and smoke from her chimney.

"Stop!" shouted George. "Stop! Thieves! Come back with that train!" But his voice was drowned by the clatter of the iron wheels on the track and the loud puffing of the engine. George leapt on to his bicycle to give chase, but he was a little too eager. His bicycle chain snapped and he fell head first into a large tub of geraniums.

George scrambled out, a large red flower poking out of his ear, and shook his fist at the departing locomotive. "I'll get you, you... you train-nappers!" he roared. He was so angry, his face glowed as red as the geraniums.

"Toot toot! Wheee!" Hugo was enjoying himself immensely. Victor, however, was not so sure. The train seemed to be going faster and faster.

"I think that we had better slow down a little," he said.

"Choo choo choo! Toot toot!" Hugo continued.

"Hugo! I said to slow down!" Victor shouted.

"Yes, Victor. At once Victor," agreed Hugo. "How?"

"How? I don't know how!" said Victor, who was now beginning to panic.

"Maybe if we put the fire out?" suggested Hugo. He opened the fire box door and tried to blow it out as if it were candles on a birthday cake. The fire roared more fiercely and the train gathered yet more speed.

"No, no, no, no, no, you numbskull!" screamed Victor.

The Tinkerbelle Belle was fast approaching a bend in the line known as the Crumbridge Curve. It was here that the course of the River Crum curved in a large semi-circle; so to avoid having to build two bridges across the river, the constructors of the Tinkerbelle Line had laid the tracks around the river bank.

As every train driver on the Tinkerbelle Line knew, the Crumbridge Curve had to be taken at a fairly modest speed. If not, the train was likely to leave the tracks and plunge into the river. Victor saw the curve up ahead and realised that they were going much too fast.

"Aaaaarghhh!!!" he screamed. And then, for good measure, "Heeelpp!!"

"What is the matter, Victor?" asked Hugo. But before Victor had time to answer, the worst happened. The Tinkerbelle Belle careered off the track, down the embankment and into the river.

"Gwibbleoobleoop!" gurgled Victor.

"Garleoogleurp!" agreed Hugo. But the train was travelling at such speed that even the river couldn't stop them. It ploughed through the muddy waters, scattering disgruntled ducks and indignant swans before it, and tore up the opposite bank. Its course had been slightly altered by its journey across the river, so that the train was now bouncing and roaring its way towards the town of Crumbridge itself.

Laburnum Avenue is a very pleasant, leafy road on the outskirts of Crumbridge. It's a quiet and peaceful road that estate agents describe as "A desirable and sought-after residential area." Nothing of any excitement happens here more than once in a blue moon.

Mrs Timmins was in her garden at number 3 Laburnum Avenue, pruning her prize roses. Mrs Timmins was very proud of her roses, and rightly so. She was hoping to win the Crumbridge Rose Growers, Association gold cup for the best roses for the third year in a row. Her cat, Binkie, rubbed against her legs and purred. In the distance, Mrs Timmins heard a deep, low rumble.

"Sounds like thunder, Binkie dear," she said to her cat.

"Miaow," said Binkie.

"Still, the roses could do with a good watering." The rumbling grew nearer.

"We'd better get inside before it starts raining," she said and, gathering Binkie up in her arms, she walked back towards her house. Just as she reached the back door, a steam engine exploded through her garden fence. Its wheels tore huge strips out of Mrs Timmins' carefully tended lawn before making a bee line for her rose-bed.

"Aaaaaaarghhhh!!!" squawked Mrs Timmins. "MY ROSES!!!" But before the words were out of her mouth, the train had dealt them a death blow. A few red petals fluttering to the ground were all that remained of Mrs Timmins' hopes of retaining the gold cup.

The train ploughed on across the gardens of Laburnum Avenue. Greenhouses splintered and crashed beneath the iron monster. Wheelbarrows, garden hoses, rakes, lawn-mowers, paddling pools, swings and slides; nothing that stood in its way remained intact.

In the garden of number 35, Mr Beesley was enjoying a snooze on his sun lounger. Mr Beesley was a very deep sleeper. (He was such a deep sleeper that he needed seven extra-loud alarm clocks all ringing at once to wake him every morning.) The sound of an approaching runaway train was certainly not enough to rouse him. Nor was the sound of his neighbours all screaming very rude words at the drivers of the train. Nor were the cries of, "Look out!" "Get up, you silly old buffer!" and "Watch out, Beesley! There's a train in your garden!"

There was indeed! And it was bearing down upon Mr Beesley at great speed.

"Aaaargh! Look out! Get out of the way!" shouted Victor from the cab. But Mr Beesley was happily unaware of all this and dreaming peacefully.

The train didn't squash Mr Beesley to a jelly. It missed him by inches, but it did just clip the end of Mr Beesley's sun-lounger, tipping it up violently. Mr Beesley was catapulted from his sleeping place, high into the air.

Bingo was played in the Crumbridge Roxy every Tuesday afternoon. It being a Tuesday, the bingo session was well under way. Mrs Timmins' sister's next door neighbour, who was was a regular player, was in a state of high excitement. She had only the number sixty-six to collect and she would have won!

"All on its own – number one!" the bingo caller shouted. He picked another numbered ping-pong ball.

"Clickety click – sixty-six!"

"BINGO!" screamed Mrs Timmins' sister's next door neighbour.

"Well, it's your lucky day and no mistake," said the woman sitting near by.

At that moment, Mr Beesley fell through the roof of the Roxy and landed in Mrs Timmins' sister's next door neighbour's lap. She screamed. (She was not used to this much excitement in one day.)

Mr Beesley woke up and looked about. He drew himself up to his full height (five feet, three inches) and with as much dignity as he could muster (he was, after all, dressed in nothing but a pair of rather large Bermuda shorts) he spoke.

"What are you doing in my garden?" he demanded. But before anyone could answer him there was a fearful crashing and thumping and hissing and banging and roaring noise from the back of the hall.

Panic took over the bingo hall as the steam train burst into the Roxy.

The bingo players screamed and scrambled to get out of the way of the oncoming train. At last, with a final hiss of steam, the locomotive came to rest in the middle of the hall amid a scene of total confusion and complete destruction.

Victor stepped down from the footplate. He laughed an apologetic little laugh. "Heh heh heh! So sorry to have troubled you."

Hugo climbed down from the train as well. "Whee! That was fun, wasn't it, my Victor?"

"No, it was not! Now come along!"

As Victor and Hugo emerged from the wreckage of the Crumbridge Roxy they were met by quite a crowd of people. There was George Sparkes the train driver, Mrs Timmins and the other residents of Laburnum Avenue, and a group of very large and very angry policemen.

"That's them!" cried George.

"They ruined my prize roses!" screamed Mrs Timmins.

"Get them!" shouted the crowd. The policemen stepped forward and placed the proprietors of Naughtiness International under arrest...

"Always you have to ruin everything!" raged Victor as he paced the prison cell where he and Hugo had been locked up.

"But Victor! It was not my fault!"

"It was your fault! It was all your fault! It is always your fault! Still, I suppose that things cannot now get any worse!" and with that, Victor threw himself on his bunk.

From beneath it came a low growl.

"Oh no..." breathed Victor, but before he could say another word, a little dog had run out from his hiding place, up Victor's trouser leg and down the other, removing Victor's underpants on the way.

"Yeearghoww!" Victor screeched.

Hugo scolded the dog. "You naughty, naughty thing!" he said. And then, a little quieter, so that Victor would not hear, Hugo giggled. "Good doggie! Hee hee hee!"